Witch-in-
Training
Broomstick Battles

Other Witch-in-Training *titles*

Witch-in-
Training

Broomstick Battles

Maeve Friel

Illustrated by Nathan Reed

HarperCollins *Children's Books*

First published in Great Britain by HarperCollins *Children's Books* 2004
HarperCollins *Children's Books* is a division of HarperCollins*Publishers* Ltd
77-85 Fulham Palace Road, Hammersmith, London W6 8JB

The HarperCollins *Children's Books* website address is
www.harpercollinschildrensbooks.co.uk

1 3 5 7 9 8 6 4 2

Text © Maeve Friel 2004
Illustrations © Nathan Reed 2004

ISBN 0 00 718524 3

The author and illustrator assert the moral right
to be identified as author and illustrator of the work.

Printed and bound in England by
Clays Ltd, St Ives plc

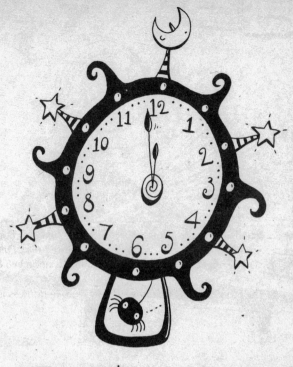

Chapter One

The clock in the hardware shop was ticking towards the witchy hour when broom riders could take to the skies. While she waited for her next lesson to start, Jessica, witch-in-training, sat cross-legged on the counter and

cleaned her broomstick. Felicity, the shop cat, snoozed on top of the Spell Books. Jessica's teacher, the legendary Miss Strega, witch-trainer and shopkeeper to the members of Witches World Wide, was thumbing through a magazine: *The Top Ten Wonders of the Witch World*. She had the look of someone who was Up To Something.

"I can't believe how much stuff has got

into my broom since I started flying," said Jessica, disentangling a long thread of her scarf from the Moon-Vault control twig.

"Achoo," sneezed Miss Strega.

"Here's a goose feather from the night we were caught in the gale."

"Achoo," Miss Strega sneezed again.

"And this dragon soot must be from Torquemada's stinking cave."

"Achoo."

"And – yeeuch! – there are blobs of sticky moondust all over the Pause and Reverse twigs."

"Achoo," replied Miss Strega, glancing at the clock.

Jessica kept on poking and jabbing between the twigs. She found one shiny gold maravedi coin, loads of scrunched-up Bewitching Jambarollie papers (from Miss

Strega's galloobious travel sweets) and some orange peel from the orchard where she had first made the Modern Witch's Pyramid Brew.

"And great honking goose feathers! This is the *exact* wand that I used to fix Heckitty Darling's ankle when she tripped over Snow White's bucket and mop. I've been looking for that for ages!"

"Achoo! Achoo!" exclaimed Miss Strega, and snapped her book shut.

"Moonrays and marrowbones, Jessica!" she said. "You really mustn't treat your broomstick like the back of an old sofa where you can stuff things. Some of us fought a war for the right to fly broomsticks."

Jessica opened her eyes wide.

"Were you in a *war*, Miss Strega?"

Miss Strega looked offended. "Not me, personally. It was a very long time ago. Haven't you heard of the Broomstick Battles?"

Jessica pondered. "Was that the war between the witches who flew their brooms the Right-Way-Up and the witches who flew their brooms the Wrong-Way-Up? I don't really know much about it."

Miss Strega tut-tutted. "That is exactly why I want you to do a Spelling Backwards project. I do believe every witch-in-training should know her witch history. Even if we lose the odd girl..."

Jessica frowned. "Miss Strega, what is Spelling Backwards? And what do you mean *even if we lose the odd girl*?"

Miss Strega stroked her long chin. "Spelling Backwards is simply going back in time to see how witches used to live in the past. It's quite easy. Returning to the present is the hard bit. One poor trainee never came back."

"What do you mean, *she never came back*?"

"Just that. She disappeared into a history book one day and no one has seen her since."

"And you can't go and find her?"

"Absolutely not," said Miss Strega, firmly. "People should never go blundering into a war zone without knowing how to get out of it."

"So, tell me, why *did* the witches go to war?"

Miss Strega blew her nose noisily. "In the old days," she explained, "when witches were wicked and had iron teeth and ate children for breakfast, *everyone* used to fly broomsticks with the bushy end behind them. Those old brooms were as good as they went, but the problem was that they didn't go very far."

"Why not?"

"Because they were powered by Sheer Bad Temper, that's why. Every time a witch wanted to fly somewhere, say to a princess's christening to put a bad Spell on her, she had to throw a hissy fit to get the broom off the ground. It was exhausting."

"How do you know? Did you fly the Wrong-Way-Up?"

Miss Strega looked offended again. "Of course not," she said. "I'm not *that* old – but

I have read my Grandma Pluribella's memoirs." For some reason, she turned a little pink and went on smartly. "However, everything changed when Dame Walpurga of the Blessed Warts came along—"

"Dame Walpurga of the Blessed WARTS?" Jessica interrupted.

"The very same. You see, Dame Walpurga, warts and all, was not like other witches. She hated eating children for breakfast or any other time; she didn't have iron teeth and she couldn't, or wouldn't, throw a hissy fit. But she *did* like the idea of flying. She used to sit astride her broomstick and do her best to get hot under the collar.

She would put her hand on her hip, purse her lips, and try to have a tantrum. She narrowed her eyes and ground her teeth. Nothing happened – Dame Walpurga was just too sweet-tempered to fly off on a handle.

So she began to tinker. Through one long dark winter, she made up a Spell for each twig on her broom – one to steer forward, one to steer backwards, another to turn left or right, higher, lower, and so on. Then, when spring arrived, she climbed up on to her roof, mounted her broom with the twigs facing her – and tweaked. Jessica, she took off! Abracadabra! Hey presto! The Modern Witch's Right-Way-Up Broom was invented."

"Hurray for Dame Walpurga!" Jessica yelled and took off on a Spin around the shop. The Spell Books went everywhere. Felicity went flying and crashed, hissing, into Miss Strega's arms, shooting murderous looks at Jessica.

Fortunately, the witchy hour struck at that very moment.

Miss Strega's broomstick came whooshing out of the Broom Cupboard under the stairs. "Come on," said Miss Strega, climbing aboard, "let's go for a *proper* Spin. I feel another sneeze coming on so there's no time to lose."

Jessica quickly clambered on to her broomstick again and whistled for her nightingale, Berkeley, to get into her pocket. Miss Strega was already disappearing through the attic trap door.

Chapter Two

Jessica landed on the tallest chimneypot on the rooftop and looked down at the High Street. Buses, cars and bikes splashed through greasy puddles. School children with violins and football kits and library books dawdled in front of shop windows looking longingly at toys and books, mobile phones and trainers.

None of them, thought Jessica, could even see the creaking sign that hung over Miss Strega's shop door.

And they can't see me, either, she thought, wrapping her Super-Duper Deluxe Guaranteed-Invisibility-When-You-Need-It cape around her.

"Do stop disappearing, Jessica," Miss Strega called from the peak of the roof tiles.

"Come over here and take my hand."

After one final chin-wobbling sneeze –
Aa…aaa…aaa…aachoooo! – Miss Strega
began to chant:

"Doog eltneg noom,
Ward su pu,
Tel su ylf,
Rafa, tfola,
Kcab, kcab,
Kcab, kcab."

At the last "kcab", a shower of bright shooting stars fell out from behind the moon. The air crackled. The whole world groaned as if some large heavy machinery were braking painfully to a halt and going into reverse. Miss Strega and Jessica teetered dizzily until the noise stopped.

All the High Street shops had disappeared. In their place lay soft rolling hills with fields of round haystacks, a river with a humped bridge, and a strange little house. Its untidy yard was stacked high with bunches of twigs

and lengths of branches.

"Tickety-boo!" Miss Strega clapped her hands. "If I'm not mistaken this is the historic site of Dame Walpurga's Well, one of the Wonders of the Witch World. Nowadays it's in the W3 headquarters at Coven Garden. Sadly, the cottage doesn't exist any longer."

Jessica frowned. "Why can we see it then if it doesn't exist?"

"Because, my little lamb's lettuce, we have just Spelled Backwards to when all the trouble started, to the witchy year of 370."

Jessica whistled. "Wow, I wish I had listened to that chant."

"What chant?" Miss Strega tapped her very long nose. "You really must be more observant, Jessica. Now, let's fly down. You'll need to turn your cape to Guaranteed Invisibility."

Jessica floated off the roof. To her surprise, the sky was filled with witches hurtling from north, south, east and west, all flying the Wrong-Way-Up on old-fashioned broomsticks. They whizzed past with centimetres to spare, muttering crossly and spitting nails. Jessica had to use both her Duck and Dive twigs to avoid bumping into them.

"Simply hopeless!" Miss Strega sighed. "Those Wrong-Way-Uppers can't even steer, let alone do any fancy flying. And, sadly, once they get tired and forget to be cross, they fall out of the sky."

Even as she spoke, one of the hurtling witches began dropping helplessly towards the river.

"Dearie me." Miss Strega gave a sort of choked giggle. "It looks like she's in for a ducking."

They hovered above the river watching until the bedraggled witch had clambered safely to the bank and joined the back of a long line of dripping witches trudging towards Dame Walpurga's cottage.

Jessica and Miss Strega zipped over them and descended beside a handwritten notice on the garden gate.

NEW BROOMS FOR OLD

Dame Walpurga was sitting on a low three-legged stool. She was very, very warty, Jessica couldn't help noticing, and even had a grinning warty toad sitting on her shoulder. Walpurga was also very, very loud. She boomed and cackled her head off as she demonstrated her new brooms to the swarm of eager customers who surrounded her.

"My first broom," she was saying, "the Walpurga Basic, had only eighteen twigs, me dears, but it's still a cracker. But you might prefer this one, the Walpurga Special. It has a Cauldron Hook, an Adjustable Seatbelt for your mascot and a very useful Air Bag (for those unavoidable crash-landings). Or perhaps," she cackled, "some of you zippier types would like the Walpurga High-flyer for some extra oomph on the Milky Way. Go on," she said encouragingly, as she passed her brooms around, "have a whirl! Have a test drive! Ig-Fo-Li, that's it. Ignition, Forward and Lift. Whoops! Re-Pa-De. Reverse, Pause, Descend. There you go!"

She roared her support as the witches hurled their old besoms away and jerkily flew up on to the roof on their new brooms. Some of them even whooped and slapped

their bottoms as they took off.

"Wey-hey!" they shouted. "Long life to Dame Walpurga and her Blessed Warts."

Dame Walpurga hooted delightedly. "Have a Spin," she yelled. "And don't forget the old Ducking and Diving."

Jessica turned to Miss Strega. "They all seem very friendly to me," she whispered. "How did they end up going to war?"

"Wait," said Miss Strega, "look who's coming now."

6

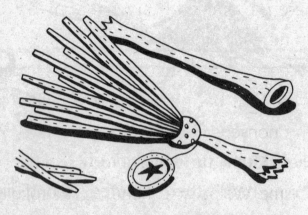

Chapter Three

As Jessica looked on, a dark figure on a Wrong-Way-Up swooped down to the riverbank. Her face was hard and scowling. She crash-landed outside Walpurga's cottage, kicked the gate open and marched up the path, pushing everyone out of her way.

"Have you come for a new broom, my dear?" Dame Walpurga asked politely. "There *is* a queue but you can have a drink from my well while you're…"

"Silence!" the witch screeched. "I am the Powers-That-Be. I have come to put a stop to this nonsense for good."

She snatched the Walpurga High-flyer out of Dame Walpurga's hands and broke it in two. Then she glared stonily at the trembling witches until, one by one, they clambered aboard their old-fashioned besoms and went screaming off into the night. Up on the cottage roof, another flight of witches zoomed off quietly on their Modern Witch's Broomsticks.

"Madam," Dame Walpurga said to the Powers-That-Be, "there is no need to be rough, no call at all for bad temper. I'll *give* you the formula for the Modern Broom if that's what you want. We can share it. I had a dream, you see. I saw a time when witches didn't have to be cross. A time when we could fly our brooms in harmony – the Right-Way-Up."

The Powers-That-Be sneered. She hurled the "New Brooms for Old" notice into the well.

"There is only ONE way to fly a broom," she screamed.

Then, in the blackest humdinger of a hissy fit, she crashed off into the night.

Dame Walpurga and her toad sat down heavily on the grass. She did not look at all jolly now.

Miss Strega didn't speak for a long time and, when she did, she spoke in a wobbly sort of a voice. "That's enough Spelling Backwards for today. We'd better get back to the shop." She reached out for Jessica's hand.

"Going, going, GONE!" she said, and waved her wand.

*

Jessica landed with a thump on the rooftop of the shop.

Miss Strega looked miserable. She didn't even answer when Jessica offered to make her a good stiff Brew.

Spelling Backwards just makes people unhappy, Jessica thought to herself. *I hope we don't have to do that again*.

And she flew straight home, without doing even one Moon-Vault.

The following evening, Miss Strega and Jessica were sitting on the rooftop having a bowl of Muncheon together. (Muncheon, as everyone knows, is the supper snack that witches eat under the moon. The marvellous thing about Muncheon is that it tastes of whatever you fancy.)

"Mine tastes of pizza margarita tonight.

What about yours, Miss Strega?"

Miss Strega sighed contentedly. "Tonight I'm having crispy duck pancakes, but you know…" She raised her glass and broke into song:

"It's not all Muncheon and Moon-Vaulting.
It's not just Mingling a Brew;
When a witch-in-training is training,
She's always got masses to do…
Always got masses to do!"

"So what have I got to do?" asked Jessica, pleased that Miss Strega was feeling herself again.

"How can you have forgotten your Spelling Backwards project?"

Jessica groaned. "I don't know how to start. I can't even remember the chant."

Miss Strega ladled out more Muncheon and poured another glass of Brew.

"A bright girl like you, Jessica, doesn't need to have everything spelled out. But you might make a trip to the Coven Garden library. Just be careful not to get too carried away by the books there. It is a witch's library, after all. Some of those books are captivating."

Jessica looked doubtful. "But what is my project about?"

"I haven't the foggiest idea, my little

cinnamon stick. I always think that if you know before you look, you can't see for knowing."

Jessica wriggled her nose. "Hang on, how can I find out something if I don't even know what I'm looking for?"

"Oh, that's terribly easy," Miss Strega replied. "I do it all the time. So do you. After all, you found your broomstick before you even knew you were a witch."

"That's quite right," said Jessica, thoughtfully chewing the end of one of her plaits. "I shall start immediately."

*

Jessica had not been back to Coven Garden, the witches' headquarters, for ages. She flew through the arched doorway and into the circular reception hall with its portraits of important witches through the ages. Their curious eyes followed Jessica as she zipped across the spider-web mosaic floor and slid up the banister stairs to the library.

She opened the door and was creeping in, quiet as a field mouse, when suddenly she heard the unmistakable sound of someone drawing in her breath and sucking her teeth.

Wishing the world well ⭐

Witches Worldwide

"Jessica?" said a voice. "Can't you see me?" A set of teeth and then a body began to take shape in front of her. It was a bit blurry around the edges but gradually became more solid, until Jessica recognised the scary figure of Miss Shar Pintake, the W3's Chief Examiner.

She peered at Jessica over her glasses and absent-mindedly poked her hair with a pen. Which was not surprising, since Jessica had once changed three chocolate mice into three head lice and left them on Shar Pintake's desk.

"I'm testing a new program for Vanishing Spells on my computer," she said, "though I seem to be having some teething problems. Are you still in training?"

Jessica nodded. "I'm doing a Spelling Backwards project."

"Really? I do hope Miss Strega knows what she's doing with these dangerous training methods. Sometimes, on quiet nights, I hear that young pupil of hers calling from the bookshelves. She seems to be completely lost in some book." Shar Pintake drew in her breath and began to disappear again, until finally there were just her dreadful teeth hanging in midair. It took a moment before Jessica realised she was smiling.

She backed away and began tiptoeing around the bookcases, starting at Alchemy and going right around the room as far as Zymurgy, whatever that was. There were Brewing books by Delia Catessen, Charm Lexicons, Encyclopaedias of Witchcraft, books about the Geography of the Night Sky and the History of Mascots, and loads of Spell Books.

"Too many books! Where shall I begin?" Jessica wondered aloud.

"Hu-eet," whistled Berkeley encouragingly.

Behind them, there was a sharp intake of breath. Miss Pintake's right arm slowly reappeared and pointed at a notice on the wall.

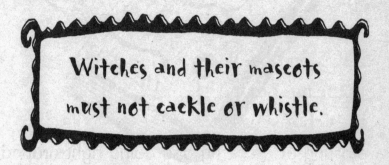

Witches and their mascots must not cackle or whistle.

Jessica pushed Berkeley down into her pocket, seized the first book to hand and scuttled over to a desk. Only then did she see the title.

"*The Story of the Besom Wars.* By Vox Libris."

She had found what she was looking for before she even knew what she was looking for!

Chapter Four

Jessica turned to the title page of her library book. She was astonished when a slow drawling voice began to speak.

"Good evening, Jessica, and Berkeley too," it said. "Welcome to my story. I'm Vox Libris.

You can stop and ask me questions at any time. You can move backwards or forwards. You can zoom into my illustrations and you can even join my chat rooms. Just be careful not to sneeze unless you're ready to travel."

What has sneezing got to do with it? Jessica wondered. She flicked through the pages to figure out where the voice was coming from. A jumble of words tumbled out.

"...cross and wanted to be boss ... in the witchy year ... Pluribella ... all-out war..."

She flipped backwards and forwards.

"...air turned blue ... horns locked..."

She closed it. When she opened it again a different voice spoke.

"Help!" said a high-pitched, tearful voice. "I'm a witch-in-training. Get me out of here!"

"Oh!" exclaimed Jessica – and shut the book quickly. When she reopened it, another stream of words bubbled up out of the pages.

"...stony-faced gryphons ... disenchantified..."

Jessica turned back to the title page. Vox Libris's calm drawl spoke again.

"Why don't you let me start at the beginning?"

Jessica nodded, wide-eyed.

Vox Libris began: "After Dame Walpurga invented the New Broom, nothing was ever the same again. For the first time in their history, witches could enjoy flying. Most of them ignored the grumpy Powers-That-Be and took to free flight like eagle chicks. Flying without having to be mad was so easy! On the old brooms, it had been hard to fly long distances, for, as you know, it's nearly impossible to stay in a bad temper for hours. But on the new brooms, witches could fly on and on and on, even sometimes as far as the Milky Way! Witch life was transformed."

As soon as Vox Libris had started to speak, Jessica was under a spell. She and Berkeley and the book were all alone in a little pool of yellow light. Music swelled up from behind

the stacks of books and moving pictures scrolled around the library walls showing grinning witches spinning among the stars.

"It wasn't long before witches invented new extreme sports like Ducking and Diving. They swooped like giant crows between snorting dragons and soared fearlessly over ash-spewing volcanoes. Muncheon clubs started up. Host covens and their guests met to exchange Muncheon recipes and swap Brewing tips. Next, Walpurga invented the Trambroom."

To Jessica's astonishment, a long multi-seated broom with a dozen cheering passenger hags suddenly zoomed over her head.

"Whoops!" she shouted and ducked, even though she knew it was just a picture that the book had conjured up.

Vox Libris chuckled. "That was especially for witches who were too old to learn to fly the new brooms themselves – Walpurga used to take parties of retired witches on night excursions."

"Excuse me, Miss Libris," Jessica interrupted, flipping over a few pages, "didn't the Powers-That-Be put a stop to all that?"

"I was just coming to that bit," said Vox Libris. The music became very slow and dark and brown. Berkeley snuggled down deeply into her pocket fluff.

"Up in her fortress in Hagopolis, the Powers-That-Be still wanted to be boss. She did not like witches enjoying themselves. She liked old-fashioned witches who threw tantrums and made repulsive Brews with mashed slug and eye of mummified crocodile. When the Right-Way-Uppers formed their own private flying club, the Broom Riders, and introduced their own driving licence—"

"Oh, I have one of those," said Jessica, swelling a little with pride.

"Well, that was the last straw for the Powers-That-Be. She called her gang together. There was a stormy meeting. Then they flew in one black hissing swarm to Walpurga's Garden. They nailed a notice to the well.

ALL WALPURGA BROOMS ARE
FORBIDDEN.
ALL NEW-STYLE FLYING IS BANNED.
BY ORDER: THE POWERS-THAT-BE

"Banned?" gasped Jessica. "Could she do that?"

Behind her, a computer printer clattered into action. Someone turned the lights on and Vox Libris's pictures faded away.

Shar Pintake appeared out of nowhere at Jessica's shoulder. "The library is closing," she said with a noisy suck of her teeth, "but you may borrow that book for one night. Just let me give you a piece of advice. Before you escape into a book, make sure you know how to get out again."

Jessica nodded gravely and curtsied at Shar Pintake who had vanished once again, leaving only her teeth behind.

"I wish she wouldn't keep doing that," said Jessica, with a shudder.

"Doing what?" said Shar Pintake's teeth.

Jessica tucked the book under her elbow and fled down the stairs.

Chapter Five

Once outside, Jessica flew up above the rooftops of Coven Garden and turned her broomstick to Automatic.

"Hurrah for Dame Walpurga and her blessed warts," she told Berkeley as she reopened her book. "If it weren't for her, no one could read and fly at the same time. On our way back to Miss Strega's, we can find out what happened when the Powers-That-Be banned Walpurga's brooms."

Vox Libris's pages rustled.

"Dame Walpurga and the early Right-Way-Uppers were truly the cat's pyjamas. They were not going to allow the Powers-That-Be to take away their new freedom. If they couldn't fly their broomsticks, well, they decided they would fly something else…"

Suddenly Jessica and Berkeley were surrounded by dozens of witches. But not one of them was flying a broomstick! Instead, they sailed past on hot-air balloons and magic carpets. Some even flapped by on clumsy stony-faced gryphons. Others had fixed themselves up with brightly painted kites or winged bicycles. There were witches bouncing along on space hoppers. One witch who obviously couldn't lay her hands on a magic carpet had bewitched her yellow-duck bath mat and had taken to the air on that.

"Great honking goose feathers!" exclaimed Jessica.

Vox Libris lowered her voice. "It has to be said the skies were chaotic. There were traffic jams, gridlock, collisions, pile-ups. And all the other sky-users, the dragons and flying horses, the tooth fairies and goblins, moaned nonstop about the newfangled traffic cluttering up the night skies."

"I don't suppose the Powers-That-Be was very happy either."

"No indeed. The Powers-That-Be never had any sense of humour. Cross and bossy,

that's all she ever was. She threw a massive wobbly. She put on a spectacular show of bad  temper. The air turned blue. She slammed doors all over the earth. She smashed plates. She ripped up papers. She stamped her feet and yelled her head off. Houses trembled. Trees fell over. A tidal wave of tantrums swept over the world. Then, she issued another decree. There's a copy of it on my next page, if you care to have a look. You might want to cover your ears. It's very loud."

Jessica Paused her broom and peered into the book. The page screamed at her.

ALL travelling is OUTLAWED. FLYING, on ANY class of broom, animal or machine, is BANNED. Any witch found outside her own witchy neighbourhood will be DISENCHANTIFIED. By order: The Powers-That-Be

"Disenchantified?" Jessica asked.

"Stripped of her powers to Spell, Charm and Brew. Expelled from Witches World Wide."

Jessica gasped. But after a moment's thought, she tweaked her Forward twig and moved off again. "So how come I'm flying?" she asked.

"Ah-ha!" exclaimed Vox Libris. "Because the Powers-That-Be was not half as clever as she thought she was. After that second decree, *everyone* was grounded, both the

Right-Way-Uppers and the Wrong-Way-Uppers, so *everyone* was unhappy. You have no idea the trouble it caused. Every witch who was abroad when the decree was made had to sneak home under Cover of Darkness. Some of them were stranded on the other side of the moon and never made it back. Others spent months flitting through forests, tunnelling underground, cycling over mountains, hitching rides on long-distance lorries. Then the dirty tricks started.

"The Right-Way-Uppers tried to ambush Wrong-Way-Uppers. Wrong-Way-Uppers put Spells on Right-Way-Uppers so that they went round and round in circles. And don't forget, there were spies everywhere. Bad fairies, sneaky goblins, owls that couldn't help hooting to the Powers-That-Be. Thousands of witches were disenchantified. Dark days…" Vox Libris's voice wobbled just like Miss Strega's the night they had Spelled Backwards.

"Go on," Jessica prodded.

Vox Libris turned over a new leaf. "By and by, all the witches turned against the Powers-That-Be. First, Dame Walpurga and the Right-Way-Uppers started the Reclaim the Skies Movement."

Jessica was surrounded by moving pictures of Walpurga and her rebel forces, Spinning and Moon-Vaulting over the roofs of Hagopolis on daring undercover flights.

"But there was great bravery on the other side too."

From far off came the sound of a low hum that gradually became a drone and then a loud angry shriek. Yellow beams of searchlights roamed the night sky. Then suddenly a party of Wrong-Way-Uppers came roaring out of the darkness. They zipped past Jessica's broom so close she could smell the smoke coming out of their ears. Dressed in short capes with sheepskin collars, leather flying helmets and goggles, they were not like any witches that Jessica had ever seen before.

"That was the famous Besoms-R-Us gang," said Vox Libris when they had passed over and the skies were silent once more. "For months they launched nightly cloak and dagger attacks on Pluribella."

"Pluribella?" said Jessica. "Was she in the Reclaim the Skies Movement too?"

"Fiddlesticks!" said Vox Libris. "She was the Powers-That-Be."

Jessica almost fell off her broom. "Never!" she protested. "Pluribella was Miss Strega's grandmother."

A little breeze rippled through Vox Libris's pages. Her voice had become a little frosty. "Who is the history book?" she asked. "Are you suggesting I'm mistaken?"

"Oh no," said Jessica, hurriedly. "But I can't believe that Miss Strega had an evil granny."

"Look," said Vox Libris, "would you like to

Spell Backwards? Be my guest. Come right in here and check the facts for yourself. All you have to do is choose the page you want to enter and sneeze the right number of times. Talk to Walpurga or Pluribella yourself."

Jessica pondered. "Unfortunately, I don't know the chant for Spelling Backwards," she said, "and, by the way, why do people keep saying things about sneezing?"

The Vox Libris explained.

Jessica listened carefully. "That sounds easy enough," she said.

"Hu-eet," advised Berkeley. She shot out of her pocket and on to Jessica's  shoulder in a shower of birdseed. Jessica picked her up and soothed her neck feathers. Berkeley had a point. It might be risky. Both Miss Strega and Shar Pintake had warned her of the dangers of getting into books. And she herself had heard that voice shouting, "Help! I'm a witch-in-training. Get me out of here!"

At the same time, it would be a shame not to try Spelling Backwards for herself. Miss Strega would be gobsmacked if Jessica met Pluribella and Dame Walpurga in person.

"Look, Berkeley," she said, "I have my lucky pebble. And I have the Safe Harbour pin that Pelagia gave me to get out of an emergency. I'll stick it on to my broom handle so that we can always get home safely. It's perfectly all right," she insisted, "we won't be in any danger. We'll try it out as soon as we get back to Miss Strega's shop."

And she popped Berkeley back in her pocket, stuffed Vox Libris under her cape and Fast-Forwarded towards the High Street.

☆ .

Chapter Six

Miss Strega was on the phone to the family witch doctor, Dr Krank, when Jessica arrived back. (Felicity had daydreamed a Spell from the book she was sitting on and had turned into a cat-shaped gingerbread biscuit.)

Jessica hopped on to the counter and began to leaf through *The Story of the Besom Wars.*

"Is that a new library book?" Miss Strega asked, distractedly eating a few stray Felicity-crumbs while Dr Krank consulted her casebook.

"Mmm," Jessica answered, thinking that Miss Strega was going to have another shock when Jessica started sneezing.

For it turned out that sneezing was the key to Spelling Backwards. All she had to do, Vox Libris had explained, was choose the time and place she wanted to visit and sneeze the Sneezing Spell. As soon as she heard this, Jessica remembered that Miss Strega had sneezed a lot the night that they went Spelling Backwards to Walpurga's Cottage. The strange chanting had just been Miss Strega being silly.

She turned to the pictures in the middle of the book. There was one in particular that looked interesting. It showed three witches sitting round a table in a dark room, lit only by the moonlight falling through a high window. Two witches wore old-fashioned pointy hats and they all wore fur-lined robes. She recognised Walpurga and the warty toad on her shoulder at once; the other had a ginger cat on her lap and, by the look of her chin and the glasses perched on the end of her long nose, she just had to be Miss Strega's grandma, Pluribella. The third witch, the one in the middle, did not have a mascot but she seemed to be wearing a set of curly spaniel's ears on her head.

Walpurga and Pluribella were dipping their long-feathered quill pens in a big metal ink pot.

Jessica read the caption beneath the painting:

The Signing of the Peace Agreement, 5th January 380.

(Left to Right: Dame Walpurga, Judge Portia, Pluribella Strega)

What an important date in witch history! The Right-Way-Uppers and the Wrong-Way-Uppers must have stopped fighting each other. And both sides must have stopped attacking the Powers-That-Be.

"Let's go and see it for ourselves. Come on, Berkeley, stop pecking at poor Felicity's ears and get in my pocket."

Then she began to sneeze, counting with her fingers.

Sneeze once for yesterday,
Twice for the century,
Three times for the decade,
And four for the year.

Miss Strega swung round. "Jessica!" she warned. "I hope you know how to come back."

Even the gingerbread-biscuit face of Felicity looked worried.

Jessica went on sneezing.

Five more for the month,
And another for the day...
Achoo-achoo-achoo!
I'm Spelling away.

The next moment, Jessica was standing on a floor like a giant checker board. She could hear raised voices in the next room. She tiptoed across the floor and peered around the thick velvet curtain at the door.

The Sneeze Spell had worked! There were Pluribella and Dame Walpurga at the table signing their peace agreement. Though it didn't sound very peaceful.

Dame Walpurga's toad was croaking at

the top of his voice; the ginger cat was standing on the table, hissing and spitting.

Walpurga herself was shouting: "I am not signing anything unless she agrees that my type of broom is the Right-Way-Upper."

"That is not fair," Pluribella shouted back. "You can call it the *New*-Way-Upper if you like, but as far as I'm concerned the old-fashioned besom was the Right-Way-Upper."

"You're wrong."

"Right!"

"Wrong!"

"Right, right, right…"

"Crek, crek, crek…" went the toad.

"Tzzzzzz, tzzzzzz…" hissed the cat.

Judge Portia banged the table with the ink pot. "Ladies, please stop bickering!"

Jessica gave a little giggle. Berkeley went "Hu-eet." Jessica clamped her hand over her mouth and stepped back into the shadow of the curtain.

Five pairs of eyes swivelled in her direction.

Pluribella tapped her long nose and rose slowly to her feet. "A spy!" she mouthed.

Pluribella's cat jumped off the table and took up a pounce-and-attack position.

Only then did Jessica realise that she had come without her broom and her Safe Harbour pin. And only then did she remember what Miss Strega had said about old-fashioned witches with iron teeth eating girls for breakfast.

She quickly turned on her cape to give

herself guaranteed invisibility and began to slowly wind herself into the curtain, round and round, until she was completely coiled up in a dark cocoon of brown velvet.

"Moonrays and marrowbones!" said a voice that sounded terribly familiar. "We know you're there! Reappear at once. I don't want to have to say it again."

"Miss Strega?" said Jessica.

She began to unwind her way out of the curtain until she was face to face, or rather nose to nose, with Pluribella, Dame Walpurga and Judge Portia. Of course, Miss Strega was not there at all.

The three witches stared at the empty space where Jessica was still hidden in her invisible cloak.

"What is it?" Walpurga snapped. "Is it a ghost?"

"It seems to know you, Pluribella," said Judge Portia. "It called you Miss Strega."

Pluribella stroked her long chin. "No, it isn't a ghost but it could be someone under an Invisibility Spell."

"Shall we toss it into our Muncheon cauldron? Or shall I just gobble it up right here and now?" said Walpurga, displaying her iron teeth.

Jessica reappeared at once.

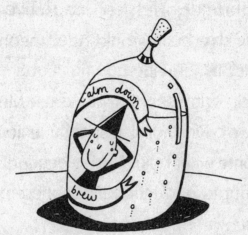

Chapter Seven

Pluribella, Dame Walpurga and Judge Portia were astonished.

"Astonishing!" they chorused when Jessica had explained who she was and why she had suddenly appeared in Walpurga's parlour.

"And you are training with my granddaughter. Fancy that!" said Pluribella, smiling broadly. (Jessica was relieved to see that she did not have iron teeth.)

"So tell us, how do you fly in your day and age? You don't seem to have a broom."

"I have a Right-Way-Upper but unfortunately I left home without it," Jessica began.

Walpurga and Pluribella leaned forwards, all ears.

"The Right-Way-Upper is which way up?" Judge Portia asked.

"It's the kind that Walpurga invented—"

Pluribella screamed. "By the screeching of peacocks and the racket of rooks, that is absolutely outrageous!" she yelled. She looked murderous.

Dame Walpurga's warts swelled with pride. Even her toad looked smug.

"Calm down," said Judge Portia. She took a moment to straighten her spaniel-ear wig, which Pluribella's yelling had knocked off-centre. "Since this Modern witch-in-training confirms that the broom riders of the future use Walpurga's brooms, the so-called Right-Way-Uppers, I suggest, ladies, that you both sign the Peace Agreement without further delay. The Witches World Wide press is waiting for an announcement."

*

So that is what they did.

Afterwards, Walpurga bustled off to declare that the Broomstick Battles were finally over and that she was the new Powers-That-Be.

Jessica stayed with Pluribella who was mixing up a Calm Down Brew.

"Are you still angry?" Jessica asked.

"On the contrary, my little apple pip," said Pluribella. "I thought the day would never come."

"But you lost the battle, didn't you?"

Pluribella cupped her very very long chin in her hand. "Listen, Jessica, I've been stuck up in Hagopolis for years with nothing but an attic full of cats for company – and some of them had disgusting personal habits, I might add.

"Every night, I had to put up with Ducking

and Diving Foursomes flinging flour bombs at me and gangs of Besoms-R-Us screeching down my chimneypots. I tried making Brews and Spells to turn them into stone or, at least, turn down their volume, but there were too many of them *and* they could all Spell back. Frankly, I was sick of the war. I couldn't wait to surrender."

"So you don't mind that the Right-Way-Uppers have won?"

"Frankly, my dear, Walpurga's broom is very convenient. It is so tiring having to get into a bad temper just to get airborne. Besides, I have had enough of being the Powers-That-Be. It's a terrible job. Let Walpurga be the boss, I say, and see how she likes all the hurly-burly. She is already quite fierce *and* she has grown iron teeth. Whereas I am much calmer." Pluribella lowered her voice to a whisper. "But don't tell Dame Walpurga I said that. Cheers!" She raised her Calm Down Brew and clinked glasses with Jessica.

"So what are you going to do now?"

"I'm planning to write my memoirs. And I'm going to study Zymurgy – that's just a fancy name for Brewing. I'm leaving Hagopolis and moving next door to Dame Walpurga here. She has everything I need in her cottage garden – I have a cunning plan to bottle her well water and sell it."

Jessica spluttered. "But aren't you two sworn enemies? That's what it says in my book."

"Great honking goose feathers, Jessica! The war is over now. We're like sisters really, Walpurga and me, chums one day, sharing a yarn and a glass of Brew, then bickering and putting Spells on each other. Mind you, we old-fashioned broom riders are not going to go away, no matter what it says in your book. Some of us will still get together and flit about looking murderous for old times' sake." She gave a little cackle. "Have you ever tried to ride the old-style broom?"

Jessica shook her head.

Pluribella's chin nodded to the corner of the room where a spiky little Wrong-Way-Upper leaned against the wall. It looked kind of cute with its lopsided twigs.

"Why don't you have a go?"

Jessica walked across and picked it up. Its long wooden handle felt warm and shiny, worn smooth by Pluribella's hands. She clambered aboard, the Wrong-Way-Up, feeling silly.

"Vroom," she said.

Nothing happened. It was just like the night of her birthday when she had tried flying for the first time.

"You'll have to get cross," said Pluribella, tapping the side of her nose.

"I don't know what to get cross about."

"Take your time. You'll think of something."

Jessica tried scowling.

She tried growling.

She narrowed her eyes and tried to look murderous. It was harder than it sounded.

These old-fashioned brooms are stupid, she thought. *Walpurga really was a brilliant inventor. The modern way of flying is much better. The Powers-That-Be had no right to be so rough; the way she broke poor Walpurga's High-flyer model broom and threw it into the well. It wasn't fair at all. And then she had the nerve to ban flying altogether! She'd been a monster, always cross and wanting to be boss, stopping people from having any fun.* It made Jessica furious just thinking about it.

"Hu-eet," whistled Berkeley, popping her head out of her pocket.

"Blithering batwings," Jessica shouted as she shot off the floor. "I'm flying." She flipped over the table, zoomed across the ceiling, zipped through the door and darted into Walpurga's garden.

Pluribella came running after her in hot pursuit.

"Wey-hey," she shouted. "Moonrays and marrowbones. You've done it! That's my girl!"

Jessica looked down...

...and remembered that *Pluribella* had been the Powers-That-Be. But she was such a nice friendly person. And so like Miss Strega. The way she said Moonrays and marrowbones. And the way she stroked her chin. And tapped her very long nose.

The broomstick came to a complete halt. Jessica hung helplessly in midair. Then she began to lose height.

Down she came, landing with a thump in the hawthorn tree. Then she toppled off on to Pluribella and knocked her over.

"Oops," she apologised, flicking some

hawthorn blossom off Pluribella's cape. "I'm terribly, terribly sorry. I hope you haven't broken anything. I started to think about Miss Strega and forgot to be cross."

Pluribella nodded her long chin in agreement. "That's the problem with the old broom in a nutshell. Staying cross is hard work. You can't allow yourself to be distracted by anything or you fall out of the sky like a stone."

"I'd better go home now," said Jessica. "Miss Strega will be worried about me. And her cat Felicity isn't well."

"Give my love to both of them. It's such a shame we never knew one another."

"I will do, as soon as I've worked out how to get back to the future…"

"Goodness, haven't you got a wand? All you do is say Going—"

"That's it!" Jessica grinned and rummaged

in her pocket. "Going, Going, GONE!" she said, and waved her wand.

The next second she landed with a bump on the shop counter. There was a lovely smell of lemons and cloves.

"Oh good," said Miss Strega, peering over her glasses. "You're back. And Felicity isn't a gingerbread biscuit any more. Would you care for some Cold Smelly Voles? I've just mingled up a Brew. I'm dying to hear all about your adventure."

Felicity gave Jessica an orange wink. She looked a little bald where Miss Strega and Berkeley had nibbled crumbs but otherwise was quite her usual self.

"I've met your grandma Pluribella," Jessica said. "She's not at all as fierce as the history books say. In fact, you are very like her, Miss Strega. The way you stroke your chin. And the funny things you say. And the way you both wear the same kind of glasses. But especially, your very very long…" Jessica stopped. Perhaps Miss Strega would think her cheeky if she said her nose was very long.

"My long what?" Miss Strega smiled.

"Your very long fingers," said Jessica, diplomatically.

"Oh yes, all the Stregas have long fingers," Miss Strega said, spreading her hands to admire them.

Chapter Eight

Next day, Jessica set off with Miss Strega to return Vox Libris to the library.

Witch history was interesting, Jessica told Miss Strega, but it was quite tricky to know how much of it to believe.

"Dame Walpurga of the Blessed Warts was *not* so wonderful, and winning the war made her horrible: she grew iron teeth and threatened to gobble me up. And Pluribella wasn't at all fierce, especially after she was able to stop being the cross and bossy Powers-That-Be. And she *didn't* have iron teeth. So you can't believe everything you read."

"How wise," said Miss Strega, bouncing off her broom at the Coven Garden entrance. "I'll wait for you in the hall."

Jessica slid up the banisters and sneaked in past Shar Pintake. There was one thing she had to do before she returned the book.

Behind the Zymurgy bookcase (Pluribella had told her Zymurgy was just a fancy name for Brewing) she scribbled a message in the margin of Vox Libris – just in case that silly lost witch-in-training should stumble on it. *Just wave your wand and say: "Going, going, gone!"* she wrote in tiny writing.

Then she slipped it back on to the bookshelf and let herself out before Miss Shar Pintake even had time to draw in her breath.

Miss Strega was standing beside a wooden signpost.

"Follow me," she announced, leading Jessica out to a high-walled garden. "I thought you might like to see Walpurga's garden as it looks nowadays and, besides, I want to buy some well water. My customers are crazy about it."

Jessica was disappointed to find that the

cottage where Dame Walpurga and Pluribella
had made their peace was in ruins. Nothing
remained of it but one ivy-covered wall. But
there *was* a model of Walpurga sitting on a
three-legged stool beside the well. And the
gnarled hawthorn tree beside it was the very
same one that Jessica had crashed into.

However, the whole garden looked very
odd. Both the tree and the well were hung
with all sorts of odds and ends. Snippets of

cloak, mini broomsticks, bird feathers, shoe buckles, scraps covered with Spells and Incantations. And when Jessica peered over the side of the well, she could see hundreds, maybe thousands, of coins lying at the bottom. There was a curious hush as out-of-town witches queued up to pat the big wart on the end of Walpurga's nose, took photos of each other at the well and decanted the water into plastic bottles.

"Why does everyone want Walpurga's water? And what's so special about that wart?" Jessica asked.

Miss Strega stroked her chin. "I expect they have read Pluribella's Memoirs. She wrote about how fantastic the water was and how drinking it could fix just about everything. So as time went by, visitors started coming from north, south, east and west to try it. Some of them want to get rid of their warts and lumps and funny bumps. Others drink it if they're sad and they want to be happy like Walpurga was. Or they drink it if they want to be inventive, the way Walpurga was. And then they leave a snippet of cloak or a coin as a sort of thank you. And they touch the wart for good luck."

Jessica snorted. "But that's rubbish. Dame Walpurga was just a very warty inventive witch. But she wasn't sweet-tempered. And the well water is completely ordinary. It isn't magic. Your Grandma Pluribella just made that up to be mischievous; she wanted to play a trick on all the Right-Way-Uppers who thought Walpurga was the bee's knees. She probably made a fortune. Actually..." She paused and looked at Miss Strega's long chin, at the glasses perched at the end of her very long nose. "...the more I think about it, you really are like your grandma, especially the way you like to play tricks. And the way you sell things that don't really work."

"Moonrays and marrowbones, Jessica, keep your voice down. If anyone heard you! I have customers who will pay a princess's inheritance for a mini-cauldron of this stuff."

She absent-mindedly patted the wart on Walpurga's nose – it was very shiny from all the fingers that had rubbed it – and began to fill a large plastic bottle.

"But there you are, Jessica, you young witches are all the same. You learn a bit of Spelling Backwards and you think you know it all."

"*Gnilleps Sdrawkcab? Doog eltneg noom?*" Jessica said casually. "Oh yes, I can do that. By the way, I saw you touching that wart for good luck. *Ti t'now krow!*"

And to the surprise of all the hushed witches in the garden, Jessica and Miss Strega began to roar with laughter.